# You Can Do It, Pout-Pout Fish!

Deborah Diesen

Pictures by Isidre Monés, based on illustrations created by Dan Hanna for the *New York Times*–bestselling Pout-Pout Fish books

**Farrar Straus Giroux**
New York

Farrar Straus Giroux Books for Young Readers
An imprint of Macmillan Publishing Group, LLC
175 Fifth Avenue, New York, NY 10010


Color separations by Embassy Graphics
Printed in China by RR Donnelley Asia Printing Solutions Ltd., Dongguan City, Guangdong Province
Designed by Roberta Pressel
First edition, 2018
Hardcover: 1 3 5 7 9 10 8 6 4 2
Paperback: 1 3 5 7 9 10 8 6 4 2

mackids.com

Library of Congress Control Number: 2017956500

Hardcover ISBN: 978-0-374-30981-7
Paperback ISBN: 978-1-250-06427-1

Mr. Fish was about to pout!
Then he had an idea.

It was a big idea.
It was a fun idea.
"I can do it!" said Mr. Fish.

“May I help?” asked Ms. Clam.

“No,” said Mr. Fish.

He did not need any help.

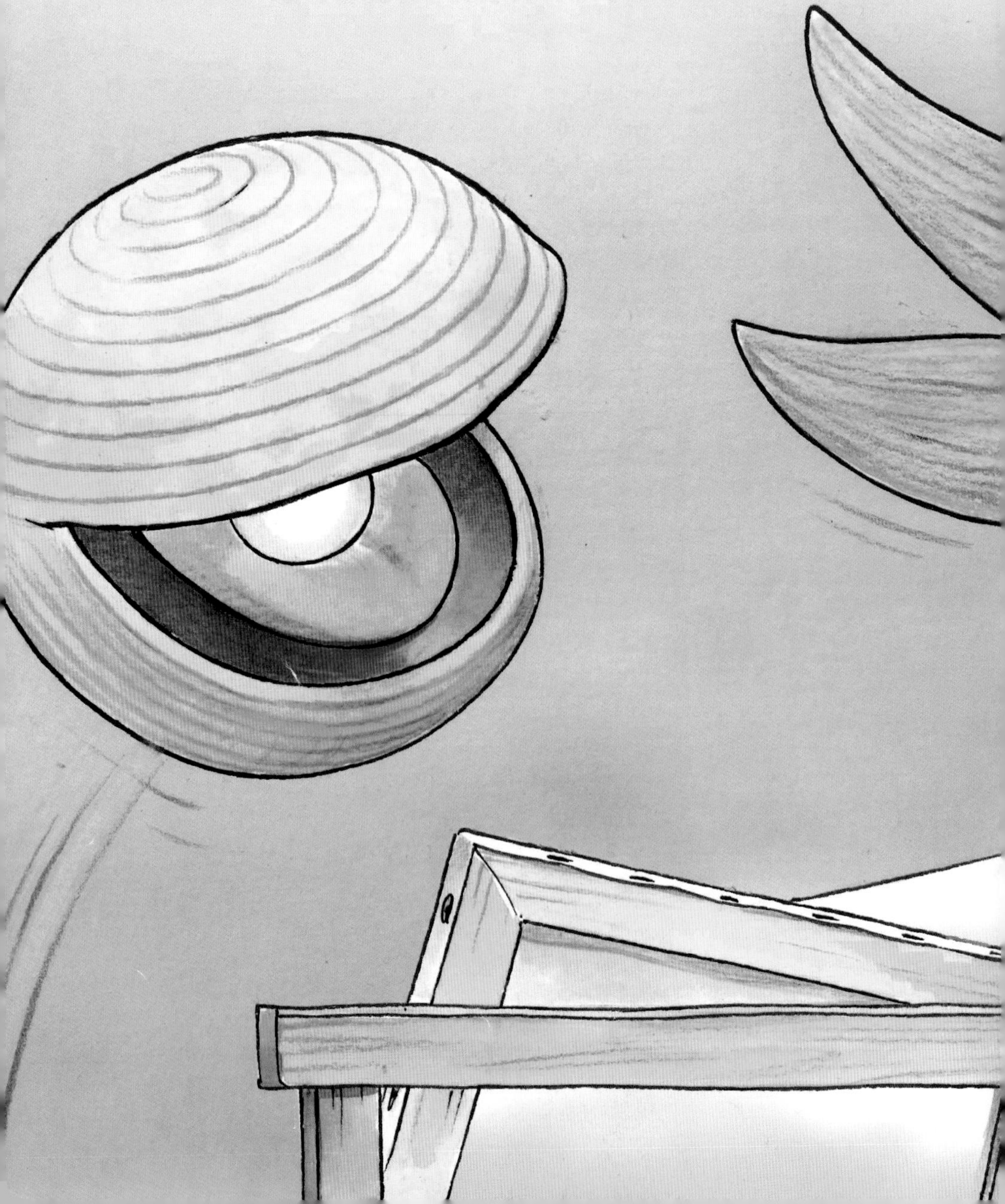

"May I help?" asked Mr. Eight.
"No!" said Mr. Fish.
He did not need any help.

“May I help?” asked Mrs. Squid.

“NO!” said Mr. Fish.

He did not need any help!

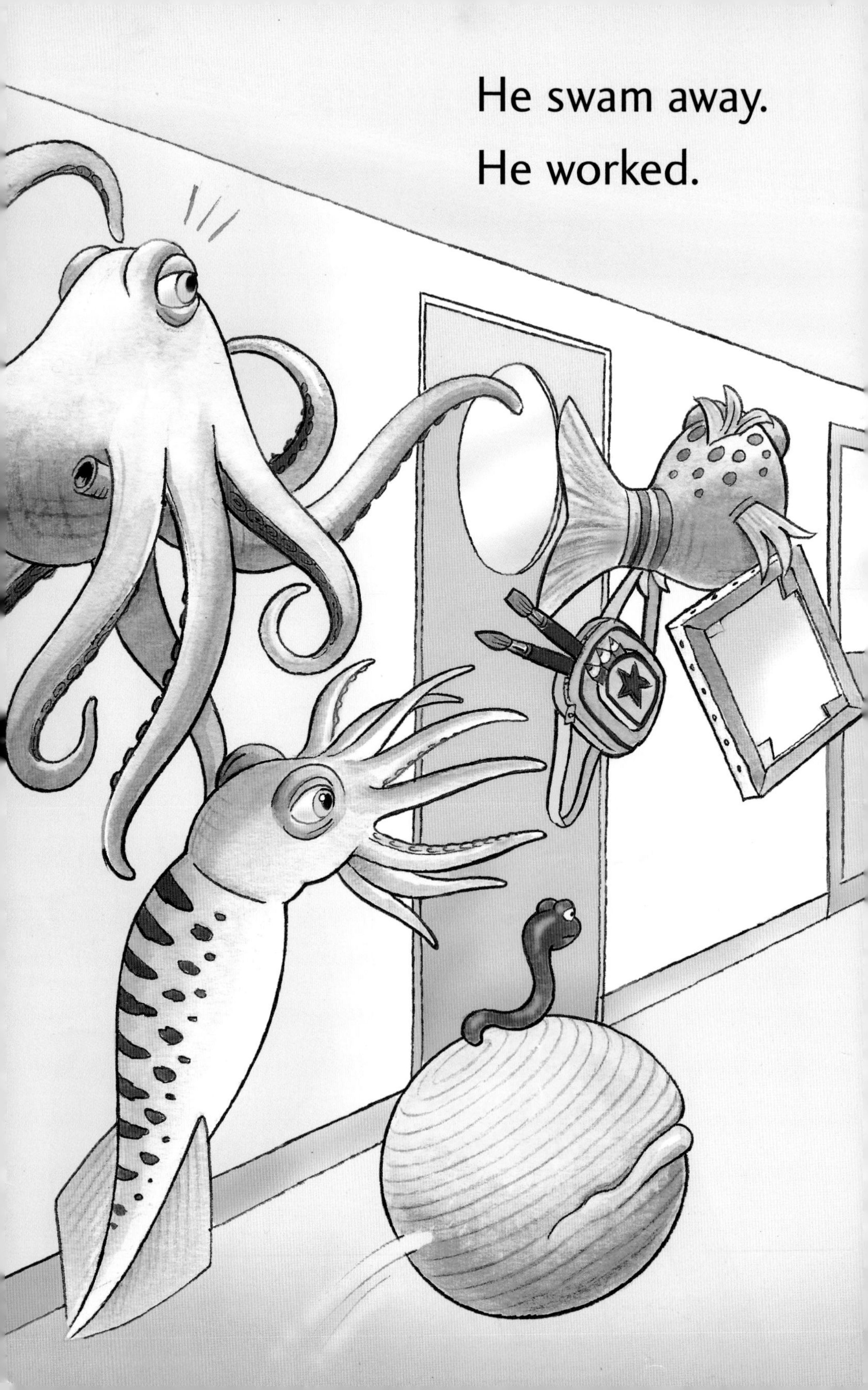

He swam away.
He worked.

And he worked.

And he worked.

But his idea did not work.
“I can’t do it!” said Mr. Fish.

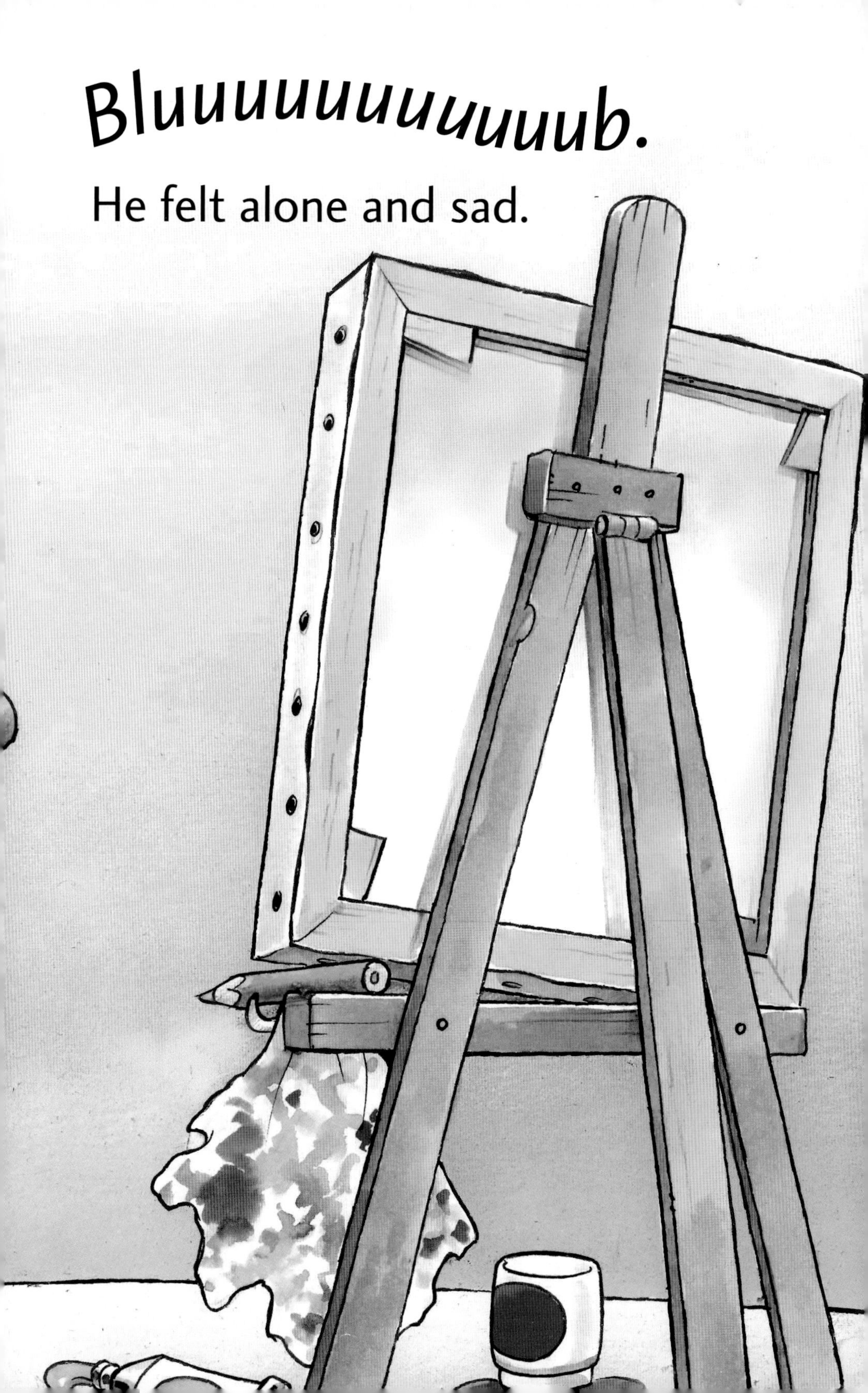

Bluuuuuuuuuuub.

He felt alone and sad.

"Yes, you *can* do it," said his friends. "You just need a little help."

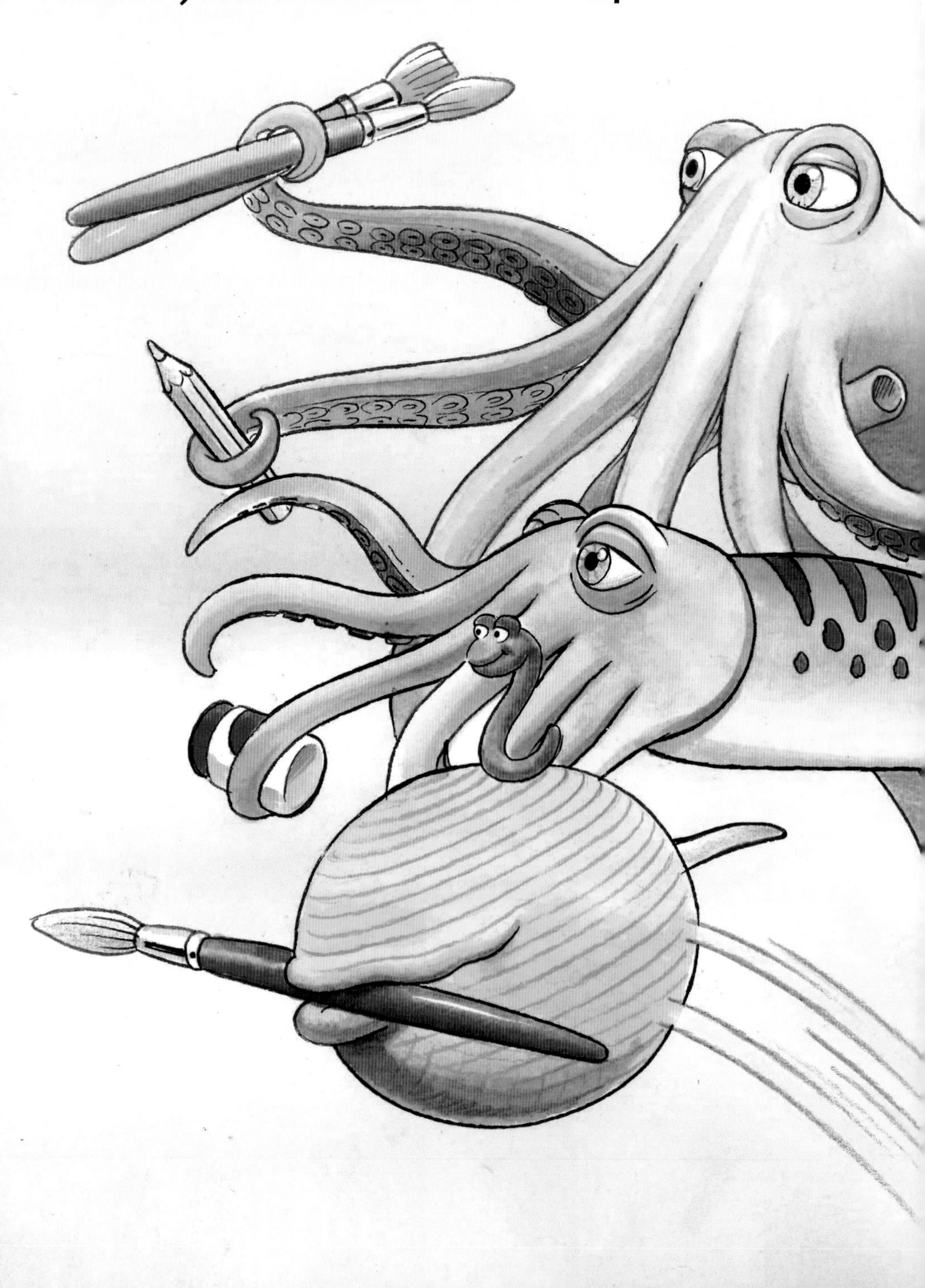

Mr. Fish and his friends
swam away together.

They worked.
And they worked.
And they worked.

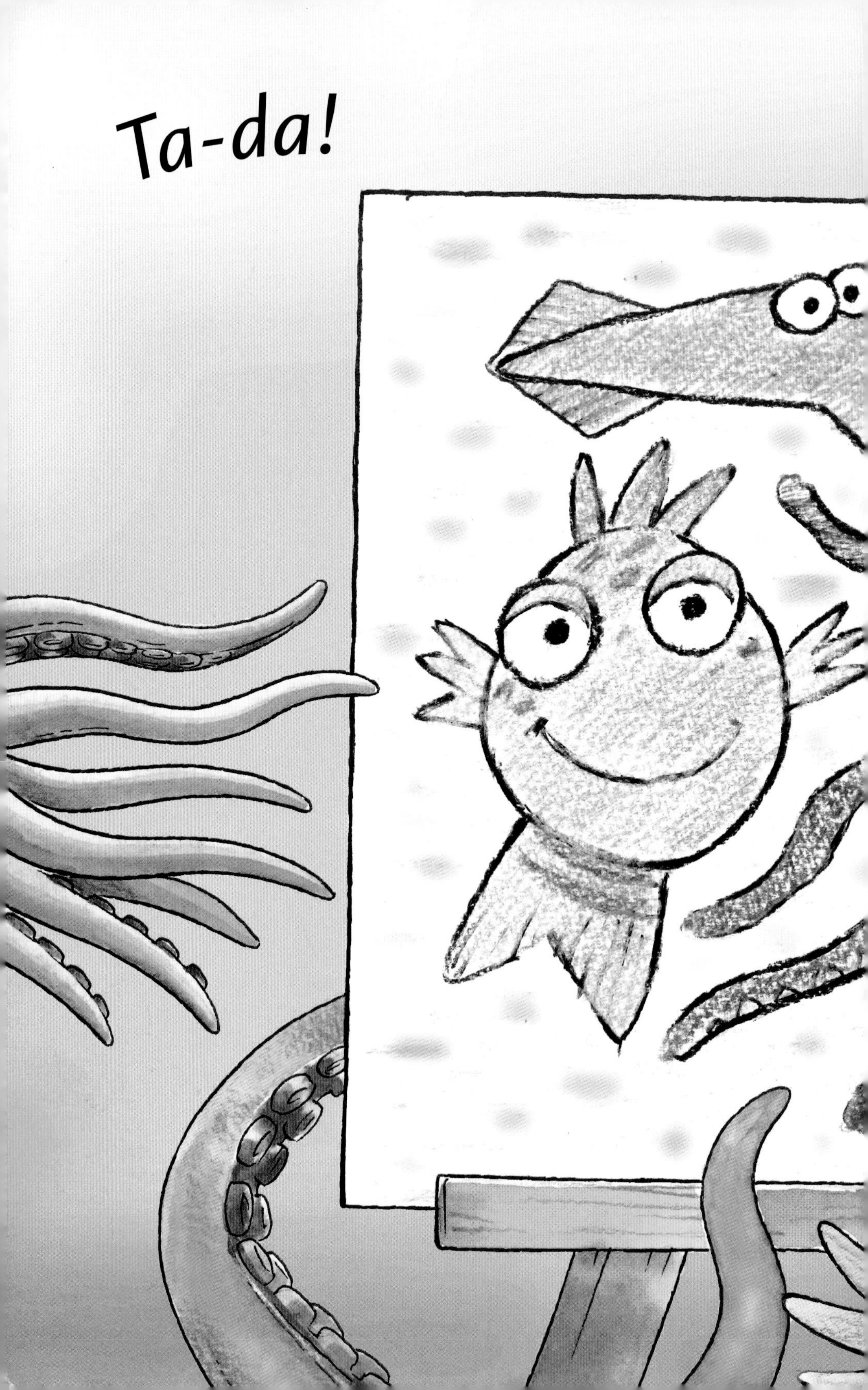
Ta-da!

"What a great idea!" said his friends.

Mr. Fish smiled.

"What great friends," he said.

“No pout about it!”